Lesley Choyce

Carrie's Crowd

Illustrations by Mark Thurman

FIRST NOVELS

The New Series

Formac Publishing Limited
Halifax, Nova Scotia

The development and pre-publication work on this project
was funded in part by the Canada/Nova Scotia Cooperation
Agreement on Cultural Development.

First publication in the United States, 1999

Formac Publishing Company Limted acknowledges the support
of the Canada Council and the Nova Scotia Department of
Education and Culture in the development of writing and
publishing in Canada.

Canadian Cataloguing in Publication Data

Choyce, Lesley, 1951-

  Carrie's crowd

  (First novels. The new series)

 ISBN 0-88780-464-0 (pbk.) — ISBN 0-88780-465-9 (bound)

I.Thurman, Mark, 1948- II. Title. III. Series.

PS8555.H668C37 1998   jC813'.54   C98-950219-8

PZ7.C448Ca 1998

Formac Publishing
Limited
5502 Atlantic Street
Halifax, NS B3H 1G4

Distributed in the U.S. by:
Orca Book Publishers
P.O. Box 468 Custer, WA
U.S.A. 98240-0468

 Printed and bound in Canada

Table of Contents

1
Is There More to Life?

Rollerblading isn't as much fun as it used to be, before Gregory moved away. Besides, my feet are growing. My toes hurt every time I put on my roller blades. And my feet always smell like peanut butter whenever I wear them.

That was because of Ernie. He put peanut butter inside my rollerblades. I haven't figured out exactly how to get back at him yet.

Ernie still hangs out with Joe down by the corner and I can tell they don't want me around.

"Why don't you go down to the library and read a book, little girl?" Joe says. I can take a hint.

My friend Laura reads books all the time. I don't see the fun in it. Laura likes reading books about space. "Did you know that Venus has clouds containing sulphuric acid?" Laura asked me one day, out of the blue.

"I'm glad we don't live there," I said.

"Nobody lives there."

"Why are you bothering to read about Venus?" I asked her.

"I just think it's interesting to know about all the planets."

That's Laura for you. Sometimes I wonder why I hang out with her.

"Did you ever dream of going into space, Carrie?"

I dream about being a kid that everybody likes. I dream about being a singer and having my own music video, but I have never dreamed about going into space. "Why would I want to go into space?"

"To explore things. It would be wild."

"Wild, yeah."

Laura put her nose back into that book again as a couple of girls walked by. It was Giselle and Kirsten. Giselle had on another new outfit. Kirsten had her Walkman turned up so loud I could hear her music.

"Don't you two ever think that there must be more to life?" Giselle said in that saucy way of hers.

"What do you mean?" I asked. She just rolled her eyes. "You know what I mean. Look at you."

Kirsten laughed really loud. They both pointed to us like there was something wrong. The other kids all turned and stared. Then Giselle and Kirsten just walked away.

Laura didn't even seem to notice. She reached into her school bag and tried to hand me a granola bar. But I saw Beth and a few other kids still looking at us and laughing.

I didn't know what to do. So I got up and started to walk away. I hate being laughed at and it wasn't even my fault.

"Carrie, what's wrong?" Laura asked.

But I didn't say anything at all. I walked. I was beginning to think that Giselle was right.

2
Feeling Like Two Cents

Just my luck. I ran into Giselle and Kirsten in the girl's room.

"No geeks allowed," Kirsten said.

"I'm not a geek," I said.

Giselle was looking in the mirror, fixing her hair. "You think my hair looks okay, Carrie?"

"I don't know. It looks like hair."

"I think Giselle's hair looks just like Sophie in the Smartgirls," Kirsten said. "You like the Smartgirls' music, Carrie?"

"Maybe," I said, but in truth I hadn't paid much attention to their songs.

"I'm going to get my hair cut really short just like that picture of Sophie on the cover of the magazine," Kirsten said.

Just then Beth walked in.

"That's a nice blouse, Beth. Where'd you get it?" Giselle asked.

Beth was surprised Giselle was being so nice to her. "My mom bought it for me."

Kirsten and Giselle looked at each other. "You mean you don't pick out your own clothes?"

"Sometimes," Beth said, looking down at the floor. Giselle and Kirsten had a way of making every girl at school feel like a fool.

"Well, at least, your mother has good taste," Giselle said.

"Not like some people we know," Kirsten added, looking at me.

Beth squinted her eyes, pointed a finger at me and gave me a look that made me feel like two cents.

All three girls went out the door and left me standing there, looking at myself in the mirror.

I hated the way I felt. Maybe there was something wrong with the mirror, but I sure looked bad. My hair was ridiculous and I wondered why I was wearing this same old ratty blouse and blue jeans.

3
Outrageous

Ernie poked his head into my room. "Why are you listening to that junk?" Ernie asked.

"It's not junk. It's the Smart-girls' first CD. It's really great."

"It's awful."

"I like it." Well, I was trying to like it.

"Shows what you know."

"Don't be ignorant."

"If I'm ignorant, what's that make you?"

I slammed the door in his face and remembered that I still hadn't come up with a good way to get revenge for the peanut butter.

I stared at the photo of the Smartgirls on their CD and then looked at my rollerblades hanging on my bedroom wall. I grabbed them and threw them under my bed. Then I started yanking my clothes off the hangers and dropping them into a pile on the floor of the closet.

I tacked the picture of the Smartgirls up on the wall, right where my rollerblades used to hang.

I was happy when my mom knocked at the door and asked if I wanted to go shopping.

"You bet," I said.

"Good. You've grown so much in the last couple of months, Carrie, that I think it's about time I pick out some new clothes for you."

"Mom, I think I'm big enough to pick out my own clothes."

"Maybe you're right."

"And I'd like to get my hair cut, too."

My mom suddenly looked suspicious. "I thought you liked your hair."

"I want hair like hers," I said, pointing to the picture on the wall.

My mom shook her head. "We'll see."

In the store I was a royal pest. The first thing I picked out was truly outrageous.

"I'm not going to let you buy that thing!" my mom said.

"What about this?"

"No way."

"This?"

"You think I'm out of my mind?"

It was all part of my plan. By the time I got to the blouse and pants I really wanted, my mom gave in. She wouldn't let me get the shoes that would match but what I bought was at least better than my old beat-up running shoes.

At the hairdresser, my mom got distracted talking to a friend she hadn't seen for a while. I was already sitting in the chair, showing the picture to the hair stylist. By the time my mom got back to me I had a whole new look.

"Who on earth do we have here?" my mother asked when

19

she finally remembered I was getting a hair cut.

"What planet is she from?" Ernie asked when I walked in the door.

"Venus," I said.

"Looks more like Mars to me."

4
The Smartgirls' Look

Laura waved to me as I arrived at the school playground but a lot of the other kids just stared at me.

I decided to ignore Laura. She never did anything but read those stupid books. Instead, I walked over to where Giselle, Kirsten and Beth were standing by the wall. I wanted to see what they'd say.

At first they ignored me altogether. It was as if I was invisible. I listened in on their conversation.

22

"Beth, sometimes I don't think you know anything about anything," Giselle snapped at her.

"But I'd get in trouble with my mother if I wore make-up," Beth said.

"I guess you do whatever your mother tells you, huh?" Kirsten said. "Not always," Beth answered.

Giselle turned to me then. She noticed my new look all right. She smiled and nodded her head up and down. "Carrie, we need your opinion on something."

"Beth thinks Cynthia Dawn is a better singer than Sophie of the Smartgirls. I say no way. What do you think?"

The truth was I still didn't like the Smartgirls' music all that much.

The lyrics were really pretty dumb, if you asked me. Giselle was waiting for me to say something. Beth had the look of a trapped animal.

"Beth's wrong," I said. "Sophie is way better."

"See?" Giselle said.

"Beth's problem is she doesn't think for herself. Probably lets her mother think for her," Kirsten said.

I could tell that Beth's feelings were hurt and I wanted to say I was sorry for not taking her side. But I didn't.

"Carrie, you want to sit with Kirsten and me at lunch today?"

"Sure."

"So who picked out your clothes?" Kirsten asked me.

"I did," I said.

"Good taste," she said. "And I like the hair."

5
Party of Friends

When my mom asked me who I wanted to invite to my birthday party, I already had my list ready.

"Aren't you going to ask Laura?"

"Um. I don't know."

"I thought she was your best friend."

"I still like her but..."

"But what?"

"It's hard to explain," I said. The truth was that everybody thought Laura was an out-of-it, boring kind of person whose only interest was books. I didn't like being seen with her. I was afraid kids would think I was like her.

"You should invite her."

"Okay."

Laura was the first to arrive at the party. "Wow," she said. "Look at all the balloons. I love balloons. Thanks for inviting me."

"Uh huh," I said.

Nobody else arrived for twenty minutes. Beth, Kirsten, and Giselle were the last to get there. They all came in together. When my mom asked them, "How are you girls today?" they all started giggling like it was a big joke. I think they thought my mom was pretty lame.

"Why all the balloons?" Giselle asked. "It reminds me of... like a little kids' party."

Kirsten took her long finger-nail and popped one balloon and then another. Then Giselle did the same.

"Hey," my mother said, "don't do that."

Kirsten popped another one and laughed.

Laura was sitting in the corner studying the bubbles in her pop. "Okay, ease up," Beth said to Giselle.

"Just trying to bring a little life into the party," Kirsten said and she stuck out her long fingernail to puncture another balloon.

"What's the matter with you, Beth?"

Beth was looking at my mother and then back at Kirsten. "I don't know. It's just not nice."

Giselle put her hand over her mouth and whispered something to Kirsten.

My mom just backed out of the room into the kitchen.

"Sorry about the balloons," Beth said.

I was looking at Giselle and she was waiting for me to say something. Instead of saying anything, I picked up a fork and popped two more balloons.

Kirsten and Giselle sort of went crazy. They knocked the rest down from the ceiling and started stomping on all of them.

Pow! Pow! Pow!

Pretty soon there were no more balloons.

Laura sat wide-eyed in the corner, eating a piece of cake.

Kirsten was looking at Beth now and then at Laura. "If I was having a party, I'd make sure I only invited kids who wanted to have fun."

Beth was going towards the door to get her coat. "I hope you like my present," she said to me as she was leaving.

I was going to try to stop her, really. But it was like my legs were glued to the floor.

"How about some music?" Giselle said.

I put on the new CD Ernie had given me for my birthday. It was the absolutely latest Smartgirls one.

"Now we can have a real party," Kirsten said, jumping up and down on the sofa.

6
Giselle Was Right

I couldn't believe that Giselle decided I was her best friend. In the cafeteria, she sat with me at lunch. "Everybody else is soooo boring, don't you think, Carrie?"

"Boring is right."

"Do you like school?"

"It's okay," I said.

"I think school is stupid."

"You're right."

"And I think they hire the ugliest teachers in the world for our school. Don't you think Mrs. Smith is ugly?"

"I guess I haven't thought about it."

"Get real. By the way, thanks for loaning me your new Smart-girls CD."

"It was a present from my brother, Ernie. When do you think you'll be done with it?"

"Who knows," Giselle said. "But don't worry."

"Okay. You can let Kirsten borrow it if you want."

"Kirsten? I wouldn't loan her twenty-five cents."

"I thought Kirsten is your friend."

"Carrie, Kirsten is, um, well, you know, boring."

"She is?"

"She's not like you."

Giselle smiled and walked away, leaving her tray on the

table. I suddenly felt like a million dollars. I saw Laura sitting by herself on the other side of the room. She looked up from her book and waved. But I didn't wave back. I thought that Giselle was so right about people being boring. If I was to make a list of boring people, Laura would have been on top. Then would come Beth. Then Kirsten.

I was beginning to wonder what was wrong with everybody, anyway.

Couldn't they see what their problem was?

7
No Geeks Allowed

Giselle's party was on Friday night. It wasn't a birthday party. "Birthday parties are for little kids," she said. "This is just a party. I'm inviting my two cousins. They know all about make-up and one of them takes modelling classes. And I'm inviting boys."

"Boys?"

"Well, not the ugly ones. Not Rick or Steven or Darrell. Just Chris and Andrew. Maybe D.J."

"Really? Sounds cool."

"We'll have really loud music. And we'll dance. You do know how to dance, don't you?"

"Sure," I lied.

"I don't know who else to invite."

"That's because everyone else is so boring. There should be no geeks allowed."

"Right. No geeks allowed."

"No Lauras."

"Good."

"No Beths."

"Excellent."

"No Kirstens."

"Like you said, no geeks allowed."

"It's gonna be the best. You don't know anyone who has the new Smartgirls CD to play at the party?" Giselle asked.

"What happened to the one I loaned you, the one Ernie gave me for my birthday?"

"Oh that. I left it on the floor of my bedroom. When I got up in the middle of the night, I stepped on it. Silly me."

"You stepped on it?"

"Well, it wasn't my fault. The room was dark."

"Oh." I felt a little funny just then because I'd hardly had a chance to listen to that CD and Ernie kept asking me about how I liked it.

"Don't worry. I think my cousin can bring hers to the party. She has everything the Smartgirls ever recorded. And wait until you see her. She looks just like Sophie."

My mom let me wear a little make-up and my new clothes to the party.

I didn't tell her that there would be boys there. The music was blasting and Giselle's parents stayed in the kitchen.

There were no geeks at Giselle's party and was I ever glad of that.

"How come I don't see you rollerblading any more?" Chris asked me.

Chris was one of the few boys in school that Giselle didn't think was ugly or boring.

"I don't know. I guess I just got tired of it."

"I don't see how you can get tired of rollerblading. I go down to the skateboard park and rollerblade on the half pipes. It's excellent."

41

"Well, I guess it is kind of excellent. You should have seen me the time that..."

So I guess you know where that was going. I really got into telling my rollerblading stories. Chris and Andrew seemed to be totally interested. Even Giselle's cousin, the one who looked like Sophie, started talking to me about the time she was rollerblading on the boardwalk in California. Wow! We were having a great time.

And then when the music stopped I looked up and saw Giselle standing by the kitchen door. She was just staring straight at me and not saying a word.

8
The Distance between Planets

I guess Giselle spent a lot of time on the phone that night. I think she said a whole lot of things to Kirsten and Beth about me, things that weren't true.

"Too bad you wrecked Giselle's party," Kirsten said to me in the hallway at school.

"I didn't wreck anybody's party."

"She'll never invite you over again," Beth said. "Why don't you go find some place to roll around on those wheels of yours?"

I thought that there must be some mistake.

Giselle was walking towards me with that sassy walk of hers.

"Hi Giselle."

"Leave me alone."

"What?"

"You know."

"Know what?"

She turned and walked away. I felt like she had slapped me on the face, but she hadn't touched me. Some kids were watching and I saw them laughing.

I went and sat down in the classroom and hid behind a book. I knew the other kids were looking at me and giggling. I felt awful and I wished that I had never gone to Giselle's party. I wished it was like before, when

I used to go rollerblading every day with Gregory.

I wished I'd never bought a Smartgirls CD or tried to wear clothes and make-up to look like them. Most of all, I wished I had never started hanging out with Giselle.

After school, I didn't talk to anyone. I didn't feel like going home. Ernie was having some friends over to play basketball and he probably didn't want me around.

So I went to the public library. I sat by the window and flipped through a bunch of movie and teen magazines. I read about all the favourite colours and favourite foods of each of the Smartgirls. All these people in the magazines had such exciting lives and mine was such a zero. What was I doing hanging around the library anyway with a bunch of stupid books and magazines? I got up to go.

That's when I saw Laura sitting with a monster pile of books in front of her. I hadn't been very nice to Laura for a while. I looked over at her, but she was lost in her books.

When I went over to sit beside her, I showed her the picture of Sophie in the magazine and said, "Did you know that Sophie's favourite food is hot fudge sundaes?"

Laura didn't even look up but she put her finger on the page where she was reading. "Did you know that the coolest part of the

sun is about 6000 degrees Celsius?"

"Sounds pretty hot to me."

"That's nothing. At the centre, the sun is more like thirteen million degrees."

"How did anybody figure that out?"

"Good question. Some day I'll be an astronomer. Then I bet I'll know the temperatures of all the stars."

Suddenly, what Laura was talking about seemed far more interesting than what Sophie likes to eat for breakfast or the fact that her favourite colour is blue-green.

"Jupiter is so far out that it takes almost twelve earth years for it to go around the sun. If we lived on Jupiter, Carrie, you and

I wouldn't even be one year old yet."

"I never knew that before."

"What do you want to be when you grow up, Carrie?"

"I thought I wanted to be one of the Smartgirls," I said. "But now I don't know."

"Don't worry about it. It takes some people a long time to figure things out. That's okay."

Walking home, I realized I didn't feel so bad after all. I knew that Laura was still my friend. And with her I wouldn't have to act like I was someone I wasn't. Maybe I didn't want to be part of Giselle's crowd after all.

The sun came out from behind a cloud just then and I looked up to watch three sea gulls flying over the library.

9
Starting All Over Again

Giselle never replaced my CD. It didn't matter though. I was tired of the Smartgirls. I think everyone else was losing interest in them too.

I was going to start rollerblading again. I started saving up to buy some new ones that fit and didn't smell like peanut butter. I decided against trying to get back at Ernie because he was being so nice to me lately. Laura said she'd like to buy some rollerblades as well. It's funny. I was beginning to lose interest in all the stuff that Giselle thought was important. In a way, I began to feel sorry for her.

Laura, on the other hand, was fun to be with. She knew about more than just Smartgirls and clothes and make-up.

One day Laura brought coloured chalk into school and we drew pictures of the planets on the pavement in the school yard. She drew Saturn really cool. Somebody walked on Mars and messed it up. I drew Earth. Round and blue green.

Beth came over and said, "Doesn't the chalk turn your fingers ugly colours?"

My fingers were pretty messy with all the colours smudged together.

I shrugged, "I don't mind, I guess."

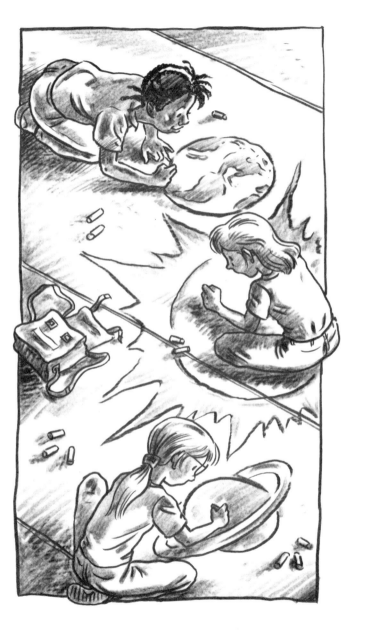

"Can I draw something?"

"You can do the sun if you want to."

"Thanks."

"Here's yellow."

Now the three of us were drawing the solar system together.

"Carrie," Beth said, "Giselle told me that you said some awful things about me. That's why I was mad."

"That was just what Giselle said. I don't remember saying anything about you."

"I know that now. I'm through with them."

"Hey, I've been there, done that," I said.

"And guess what? Kirsten just found out that she's moving."

"I guess Giselle isn't going to have many friends left."

"Did you know the Smartgirls just broke up. No more CDs," Beth announced. She was full of surprises.

"Wow. Did you hear that, Laura?"

Laura was busy finishing up the ring around Saturn. "Uh-huh." When she finished up with Saturn's rings, she handed what was left of her piece of yellow chalk to Beth. Beth had run out of chalk because the sun is so big.

"Do you believe there is intelligent life on other worlds?" Laura asked me.

"I don't know," I answered. "I hope so. What do you think, Beth?"

Beth accidentally smeared a big streak of yellow chalk across her face and looked up at the real sun in the sky above us. "Yes," she said. "I'm one hundred per cent sure."

When it rained that afternoon, none of us minded very much that the solar system disappeared from the school yard. We decided that we would start it all over again on Monday.

About the Author...

LESLEY CHOYCE is the author of 43 books of poetry, non-fiction and fiction for adults and children, as well as *Carrie's Crowd* and *Go For It, Carrie*. His writing has earned him two Dartmouth Book Awards and the Ann Connor Brimer Award for the novel *Good Idea Gone Bad*. Many of his books have received the Canadian Children's Book Centre's "Our Choice" Award.

About the Illustrator...

MARK THURMAN is a writer and illustrator living half the year in Toronto and the other half in Owen Sound, Ontario. He has written and illustrated over 25 books for children, as well as *Carrie's Crowd* and *Go For It, Carrie* and the series *Douglas and the Elephant*.

Another story about Carrie...

• *Go For It, Carrie*
by Lesley Choyce/Illustrated by Mark Thurman
More than anything else, Carrie wants to
roller-blade. Her big brother and his friend
just laugh at her. But Carrie knows she can
do it if she just keeps trying. As her friend
Gregory tells her, "You can do it, Carrie. Go
for it!"

Meet five other great kids in the New First Novels Series...

Meet Morgan in

• *Morgan and the Money*
by Ted Staunton/Illustrated by Bill Slavin
When money for the class trip goes
missing, Morgan wonders who to tell
about seeing Aldeen Hummel, the Godzilla
of Grade 3, at the teacher's desk with
the envelope. Morgan only wants to do
the right thing, but it's hard to know if not
telling all the truth would be the same as
telling a lie.

• *Morgan Makes Magic*

by Ted Staunton/Illustrated by Bill Slavin
When he's in a tight spot, Morgan tells stories — and most of them stretch the truth, to say the least. But when he tells kids at his new school he can do magic tricks, he really gets in trouble — most of all with the dreaded Aldeen Hummel!

Meet Jan in

• *Jan and Patch*

by Monica Hughes/Illustrated by Carlos Freire
Jan wants a puppy so badly that she would do just about anything to get one. But her mother and her gramma won't allow one in the house. So when Jan and her friend Sarah meet a puppy at the pet store, they know they have to find a creative way to make him Jan's.

• *Jan's Big Bang*

by Monica Hughes/Illustrated by Carlos Freire
Taking part in the Science Fair is a big deal for Grade 3 kids, but Jan and her best friend Sarah are ready for the challenge. Still, finding a safe project isn't easy, and the girls discover that getting ready for the fair can cause a whole lot of trouble.

Meet Lilly in

• *Lilly's Good Deed*

by Brenda Bellingham/Illustrated by
Kathy Kaulbach

Lilly can't stand Theresa Green. Now she
is living on Lilly's street and making
trouble. First, Lilly's friend Minna gets
hurt because of Theresa's clumsiness, then
Lilly is hurled off her bike when Theresa
gets in the way. But when they have to
work together to save the life of a kitten,
Lilly has a change of heart.

• *Lilly to the Rescue*

by Brenda Bellingham/Illustrated by
Kathy Kaulbach

Bossy-boots! That's what kids at school start
calling Lilly when she gives a lot of advice
that's not wanted. Lilly can't help telling
people what to do — but how can she keep
any of her friends if she always knows better?

Meet Robyn in

• *Robyn's Want Ad*

by Hazel Hutchins/Illustrated by
Yvonne Cathcart

Robyn is fed up with being an only child.
She decides that having a part-time brother

would be ideal. But the only person who answers her classified ad is her neighbour Ari and he wants Robyn to teach him piano. All she wanted was a brother, plain and simple, and now she's mixed up in Ari's plot to avoid his real piano lessons.

• *Shoot for the Moon, Robyn*

by Hazel Hutchins/Illustrated by Yvonne Cathcart

When the teacher asks her to sing for the class, Robyn knows it's her chance to be the world's best singer. Should she perform like Celine Dion, or do *My Bonnie Lies Over the Ocean*, or the matchmaker song? It's hard to decide, even for the world's best singer — and the three boys who throw spitballs don't make it any easier.

Meet Duff in

• *Duff the Giant Killer*

by Budge Wilson/Illustrated by Kim LaFave

Getting over the chicken pox can be boring, but Duff and Simon find a great way to enjoy themselves — acting out one of their favourite stories, *Jack the Giant Killer*, in the park. In fact, they do it so well the police get into the act.

Look for these First Novels!

• *About Arthur*
Arthur Throws a Tantrum
Arthur's Dad
Arthur's Problem Puppy

• *About Fred*
Fred and the Flood
Fred and the Stinky Cheese
Fred's Dream Cat

• *About the Loonies*
Loonie Summer
The Loonies Arrive

• *About Maddie*
Maddie in Trouble
Maddie in Hospital
Maddie Goes to Paris
Maddie in Danger
Maddie in Goal
Maddie Wants Music
That's Enough Maddie!

• *About Mikey*
Mikey Mite's Best Present
Good For You, Mikey Mite!
Mikey Mite Goes to School
Mikey Mite's Big Problem

• *About Mooch*
Mooch Forever
Hang On, Mooch!
Mooch Gets Jealous
Mooch and Me

• *About the Swank Twins*
The Swank Prank
Swank Talk

• *About Max*
Max the Superhero

• *About Will*
Will and His World

Formac Publishing Company Limited
5502 Atlantic Street, Halifax, Nova Scotia B3H 1G4
Orders: 1-800-565-1975 Fax: (902) 425-0166